Pippa
the Poppy
Fairy

by Daisy Meadows

SCHOLASTIC INC.

New York   Toronto   London   Auckland   Sydney
Mexico City   New Delhi   Hong Kong   Buenos Aires

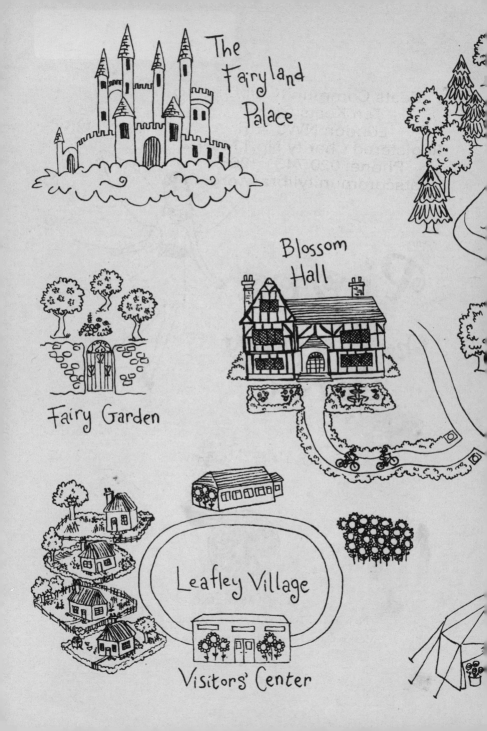

I need the magic petals' powers,
To give my castle garden flowers.
I plan to use my magic well
To work against the fairies' spell.

From my wand ice magic flies,
Frosty bolts through fairy skies.
This is the crafty spell I weave
To bring the petals back to me.

Contents

Special Delivery

"I love Blossom Hall!" Kirsty Tate
sighed happily as she finished off a
delicious bowl of fruit and cereal.

She was sitting on the sunny
terrace of the hotel restaurant with her
best friend, Rachel Walker, and their
parents. The two families were spending
spring break at the beautiful old

mansion that was now a hotel. The sky was blue, and the pink-and-white cherry trees in the gardens were in full bloom.

"It's so pretty," Rachel agreed.

"Did you find the Fairy Garden yesterday?" Mrs. Tate asked.

Rachel and Kirsty nodded.

"It was magical!" Rachel said. She and Kirsty grinned at each other.

The two girls shared a very special secret. On their first vacation together, they had become friends with the fairies. And yesterday, they had met Tia the Tulip Fairy in the hotel garden, and they started a whole new fairy adventure!

"What do you two want to do today?" asked Mr. Walker.

"We'd like to explore inside Blossom Hall," Rachel said eagerly.

"I can't wait to look around," Kirsty added. "Mom, can we please —"

"Yes, you can leave the table if you're finished." Mrs. Tate laughed.

"All the more bacon and eggs for me!" Mr. Walker joked as the girls got up.

Laughing, Rachel and Kirsty left the restaurant and headed down one of the winding hallways. They looked at the pictures on the walls.

One of the pictures showed a pretty village green. "That's Blossom Village, isn't it?" Kirsty said.

Rachel nodded. They had driven through the village to reach Blossom Hall.

"This is Blossom Hall a long time ago," Rachel remarked, pausing in front of another print.

Next to the picture of Blossom Hall was an oil painting of a field sprinkled with wildflowers: scarlet poppies, golden buttercups, and blue cornflowers.

"It's a good thing they're only painted flowers," Rachel sighed. "All of the real flowers are dying now that the Petal Fairies' magic petals have been stolen!"

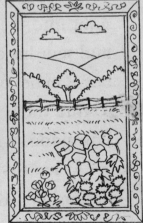

The girls had learned that Jack Frost
was causing trouble for the fairies again.
He had sent his goblins to steal the seven
magic petals. Without the petals, flowers
in Fairyland and in the human world
could not bloom properly. The Petal
Fairies had tried to get their petals back,
but when their magic collided with Jack
Frost's icy spell, the petals spun out of
sight into the human world. Jack Frost
had sent his goblins to bring them back,
but Rachel and Kirsty were determined
to find the petals first and return them to
Fairyland, where they belonged.

"At least we found Tia's tulip petal
yesterday," Kirsty said. "I wonder if we'll
find another magic petal today."

"I hope so," Rachel replied.

The girls arrived in the hotel lobby, a spacious room with stained glass windows and a large wooden table that held a pretty flower arrangement. Just then, the main doors opened and a man in a blue uniform came in, carrying an enormous basket of flowers.

"Hello, Bill," said Jenny, the receptionist. "Can you put the flowers in their usual spot, please?"

Bill went over to the table, removed the old basket of dying flowers, and put the new one in its place. Rachel thought the flowers were beautiful, especially the huge poppies. Their silky petals were rich shades of red and orange, which contrasted with their jet-black centers.

Bill walked over to the reception desk and began to discuss the next week's order with Jenny. Rachel and Kirsty could see that he had *Petal Perfection Flower*

Shop printed on the back of his uniform.

"That's the flower shop in Blossom Village," Kirsty said to Rachel. "We drove past it on our way here."

"We'll do our best, Jenny," Bill was saying, "but we're having a lot of problems lately. Our flowers are dying very quickly — and we don't know why!"

Kirsty sighed. "It's because six of the seven magic petals are still missing," she whispered to Rachel. "New flowers won't grow, and the ones that have

already bloomed don't last very long at all."

Rachel nodded sadly.

Bill took out his notebook. "I'll go and get the rest of the order from the hotel manager," he said, hurrying off.

Rachel stared at the flowers Bill had just brought in. She could see that some of them were already wilting, even though they were fresh from the flower shop. Suddenly, her heart skipped a beat.

"Kirsty," she whispered, clutching her friend's arm, "I just saw some red fairy sparkles shoot out of the basket!"

"Oh!" Kirsty looked thrilled.

The two girls hurried over to the flowers. As they reached them, there was another shower of crimson sparkles, and a tiny fairy zoomed out from the middle of a scarlet poppy.

A Window Seat

"Oh, girls, I'm so glad to see you!"
Pippa the Poppy Fairy exclaimed. Pippa
danced through the air toward Kirsty
and Rachel. She wore a floaty scarlet
dress, a matching headband, and tiny
ballet shoes decorated with poppies.

"Hello, Pippa," Kirsty said excitedly.
"Do you think your magic petal's here?"

Pippa's glittering wings drooped a little. "No, it's not here," she said sadly. "But I know where it is!" "Tell us, Pippa." Rachel encouraged the little fairy. "Well, I was in the flower shop in Blossom Village, looking for my petal," Pippa explained. "But I was so busy looking that I got swept up in this basket of flowers and carried out of the shop!" "So that's how you ended up here," said Kirsty.

Pippa nodded. "And I'm glad you and Rachel found me," she added, "because I didn't know where I was going. But I'm sure I saw my magic petal just as I got carried out of the shop. I have to get back there as soon as I can!"

Kirsty and Rachel glanced around cautiously. The lobby was getting very busy as people passed through on their way to and from breakfast.

"Let's go over to the window seat and
come up with a plan,"
Rachel suggested.

Pippa nodded and
dived into Rachel's
pocket. Then the girls
hurried over to the
large bay window
and sat down on the
velvet cushions.

"Look at my poor poppies," Pippa
said, peeking out and pointing at the
basket of flowers. Rachel and Kirsty could
see that the delicate
blooms were
already starting
to droop.

"My magic
petal helps the

poppies and all the other red flowers
grow. I must get the poppy petal back, so
the red flowers can bloom again!"

"The tulips are beautiful,"
Kirsty remarked, gazing at
the orange flowers, which
were bold and bright.
"That's because we
found Tia the Tulip
Fairy's petal
yesterday."

Pippa nodded.
"All of the magic
petals must be safely
back in Fairyland before all the flowers
will be able to grow properly again," she
pointed out.

"We'll find them," Rachel said in a
determined voice.

"Don't forget that the goblins have a wand full of Jack Frost's icy magic to help them," Pippa said with a shiver. "We must be careful, girls."

Kirsty nodded, but just then a movement outside the window caught her eye. She turned to look. There was a big, green goblin running at full speed across the hotel courtyard!

"Look, it's a goblin!" Kirsty gasped.

The goblin was running toward a white van parked outside the hotel. *Petal Perfection*

Flower Shop was painted on the side of the van in curly green letters, and its back doors were wide open. As the girls and Pippa watched, the goblin skidded to a halt and waved his arms. A whole band of goblins raced out of the bushes! One of them was carrying the glittering icy wand that Jack Frost had given them.

"There are lots of them!" Pippa whispered anxiously as the goblins began climbing onto each other's shoulders to get inside the van.

"They're looking for the magic petal," Rachel replied.

Pippa shook her head. "It's still at the flower shop. I'm sure of it," she said.

"Look at what the goblins are doing now!" Kirsty whispered, frowning.

All the goblins had climbed inside the
delivery van. The girls and Pippa
couldn't see them, but they *could* see
flowers flying out of the open doors of
the van. Daffodils, tulips, and other
flowers came hurtling out, landing in a
messy pile in the courtyard.

"Oh!" Pippa cried, clasping her hands
together. "How can they treat those
beautiful flowers like that? We have to
stop them!"

"Yes, and quickly, too," Rachel added
anxiously. "Before the delivery man
sees them!"

Goblins
Get a Ride

Quickly, Pippa snuggled down inside Rachel's pocket again, and the two girls jumped up. But they were too late! Bill was already at the hotel door, waving good-bye to Jenny.

"I'll take your order straight back to the shop," he was saying. "Good-bye!"

Kirsty and Rachel glanced at each other as Bill stepped outside. They rushed into the courtyard after him and were just in time to see him picking up the flowers that were scattered on the ground.

"What happened here?" Bill muttered. "The wind couldn't have blown the flowers out of my van. I must have knocked them over when I got the hotel's order out."

The girls watched as Bill carefully loaded the flowers back into the van and closed the doors. They couldn't see a single goblin.

"Do you think the goblins jumped out before Bill got here?" whispered Rachel.

"I don't know," Kirsty said, frowning.

Bill climbed into the van and, with a cheery wave to the girls, he drove off.

"Kirsty!" Rachel cried suddenly. "Look at the back of the van!"

Kirsty's heart sank. There, grinning at them from the back windows of the flower truck, were the goblins! They were making faces at Pippa and the girls, sticking their tongues out and wagging their fingers behind their ears. As the van pulled away, they waved good-bye, looking very happy with themselves.

"The goblins are on their way to the flower shop," Rachel groaned.

"They might even find Pippa's magic petal!" added Kirsty.

"I don't want to think about all the damage those awful goblins could do in the flower shop," Pippa said. "Girls, we have to go after them!"

"I'm sure our parents will let us go to the village," said Kirsty. "It's just at the end of the hotel driveway."

"But we'll need a reason to go to the flower shop," Rachel pointed out.

Kirsty nodded thoughtfully. At that moment, she noticed a crumpled piece of paper lying on the gravel driveway. She picked it up.

"What's that?" asked Rachel curiously.

Kirsty smoothed out the paper. Across the top, she could see the words, "Petal Perfection Flower Shop, High Street, Blossom Village." There was some writing underneath.

"One basket of pink roses, one bouquet of pink-and-white tulips," Kirsty read out loud. "This is the hotel's order for next week. Bill must have dropped it."

"Perfect!" Rachel beamed happily. "We can go to the flower shop to return it."

Pippa was so excited, she

twirled out of
Rachel's pocket
in a shower of
red sparkles.
"Hurry, girls!"
she said eagerly.
"You'd better go
and ask your parents'
permission."

"I'll do that," Rachel
replied. "Maybe we could borrow
some of the hotel's bikes, Kirsty. The
driveway's really long, and riding would
be much faster than walking."

"Good idea," Kirsty agreed. The
girls knew that Blossom Hall kept
bicycles for guests to use to explore the
countryside. "I'll go into the lobby and
ask Jenny."

"I'll wait here," Pippa said, zooming out of sight behind a nearby bush.

Rachel hurried off to find their parents while Kirsty went back into the hotel lobby to talk to Jenny.

"Of course you can borrow some bikes, Kirsty," Jenny said kindly. "Come with me."

The receptionist took Kirsty to a large garage behind the hotel where the bikes were stored. She gave Kirsty padlocks and chains for the bikes, and two helmets. Then she helped Kirsty wheel the bikes around to the hotel driveway, before returning to the reception desk.

"That was quick!" Pippa whispered,
popping out of the bushes as soon as
Jenny had disappeared.

"And here comes Rachel," said Kirsty.

"We can go," Rachel announced, "but
we can't leave the village and we have
to be back in an hour."

Pippa immediately flew into the basket on the front of Rachel's bike and settled down comfortably. "Let's go," she cried. "We don't have a moment to lose!"

Petal Pandemonium

The girls put on their helmets, climbed onto the bikes, and pedaled off as fast as they could. The driveway was long and winding, and soon Rachel and Kirsty were breathing hard.

"Look at the fields," Pippa pointed out, as the gates at the end of the driveway finally came into view. "Even my beautiful wild poppies are dying!"

Rachel and Kirsty could see that the scarlet poppies were wilting. Not only that, but many of the primroses and snapdragons in the field were dying, too, even though they were supposed to be in full bloom.

"We have to get all the magic petals

back," said Rachel in a determined voice, forcing herself to pedal faster.

The Petal Perfection Flower Shop was on High Street near the village green.

"Let's hope the goblins haven't found my magic petal yet," Pippa whispered as she slipped into Rachel's pocket.

Kirsty and Rachel locked up their bikes, took off their helmets, and hurried into the shop. Nobody was inside except for a woman standing behind the counter. Her long dark hair was pulled back in a ponytail, so the girls could easily see that she was

frowning. She shook her head as she put
blue irises and yellow roses together in a
beautiful arrangement.

"Oh, dear!" The woman sighed
as she laid aside a drooping rose. Then she
spotted Rachel and Kirsty. "Hello,"
she said, looking flustered. "Sorry, I
didn't see you there. I'm having some
problems with my flowers."

Rachel and Kirsty glanced around the
shop. They could see that there were
many flowers on display in tall silver
vases, and they were almost all

looking sad and bedraggled. The poppies
were especially bad, their stems
bending and their thin petals
withering at the edges.

"We have lots of
orders to fill. I don't
know how I'm going to
manage," the woman went
on. "Anyway, I'm Kate. My
husband, Bill, and I own the
shop. What can I do for you?"

"We're staying at Blossom Hall,"
Kirsty explained, holding out the piece of
paper. "Bill came in this morning with
the flowers, but he accidentally dropped
next week's order when he left."

Kate smiled at them. "Oh, thank you,
girls," she said gratefully. "Bill got back a
little while ago, but he just took the van

to deliver another
order."

Rachel and Kirsty
glanced at each
other. They
wondered if the
goblins had
managed to escape
from the van and
get into the shop.

"I need to finish this bouquet for a new
mom," Kate explained. "But why don't
you go through to the back room and
choose some flowers to take home as a
thank you?"

"Sure!" Rachel and Kirsty chorused.

Kate pointed at a door behind the
counter. "It's through there," she said.
"Just help yourselves."

"Perfect!" Pippa whispered, peeking her head out of Rachel's pocket as soon as the girls had closed the door behind them. "Now we'll have a chance to look for my magic petal!"

"And maybe for the goblins, too," added Kirsty.

Quickly, the girls and Pippa hurried into the back room.

"Oh, no," Rachel groaned, freezing in the doorway. "The goblins are here!"

The goblins were running around,

frantically looking for the magic petal.
The room was a complete mess!
Pippa and the girls stared at
the buckets of flowers that
had been kicked over,
and at the spilled
water on the floor.
There were stray
petals and leaves
everywhere.

But the goblins
were having a lot
of fun! One had
wrapped himself in
a roll of pink,
flowery wrapping
paper. He looked like an
Egyptian mummy, with just his
big green ears, nose, and feet

sticking out. Another had draped
himself in colorful ribbons
and was swinging another
long ribbon over his
head like a lasso.
The goblin with the
wand had
a large daffodil
stuck behind
each ear and
a garland of
daisies around
his neck.
"I don't think
they've found
the petal yet,"
Kirsty whispered.
She, Rachel, and Pippa
couldn't help laughing

at the goblins'
antics, even
though they
were horrified by
the mess.

"No, they're
having too much
fun!" Rachel
replied. "Look,
one's stuck!"

The biggest
goblin was
upside-down in an
empty flower bucket,
his arms and legs waving in the air.
He was yelling loudly, but his voice was
muffled, so nobody could hear what he
was saying.

Pippa and the girls watched as two other goblins grabbed his legs and yanked him out.

As his head came out of the bucket, the girls could see that he was grinning. "I found the magic petal!" he shouted triumphantly.

Ice Magic

Rachel, Kirsty, and Pippa stared as the goblin held up a beautiful scarlet poppy petal.

"I'm going to take it straight to Jack Frost!" he boasted.

"No, I want to!" one of the others yelled. All the other goblins immediately joined in, trying to grab the fragile petal.

Rachel couldn't watch! The goblins could easily rip the petal apart. "Give that back!" she demanded bravely. The goblins all turned to glare at her.

"I don't think so!" the biggest goblin sneered. He dashed out of the back door of the shop, followed by all the other goblins.

"We can't follow them or Kate will wonder where we've gone," Rachel said. "We'd better go out the front door."

"Can you clean up this mess, Pippa?" asked Kirsty.

Quickly, Pippa waved her wand and a shower of fairy sparkles magically cleared up the whole room, rolling up the wrapping paper and ribbons, and putting the flowers back into their buckets.

"I can't make the wilting flowers bloom properly, though. Not without my magic petal." Pippa sighed, fluttering back into Rachel's pocket.

The two girls raced back into the shop.

Kate looked at them in surprise. "Didn't you find any flowers you liked?" she asked.

"We, um, just remembered something we have to do in the village first," Kirsty stammered.

"We'll come back later to get some flowers, if that's OK," added Rachel.

"That's fine," Kate replied.

The girls quickly unlocked their bikes and pedaled around to the back of the store.

"There they go!" Rachel shouted, catching a glimpse of the goblins running into the park. The girls pedaled after them. But by the time they had biked

into the park, the goblins were nowhere
to be seen.

"They must be here somewhere,"
Kirsty said. She gazed around as they
came to a stop underneath an oak
tree. She could see trees and
flowerbeds, and a hill nearby, but no
goblins.

Ssshhh!

The sound
came from above,
startling Kirsty. She
glanced up and saw
a very odd-looking
green branch. Kirsty
clapped a hand to
her mouth as she
realized that it was
a goblin's leg!

As quietly as she could, she got off her bike, tapped Rachel on the shoulder, and pointed upward. Rachel and Pippa saw the leg, and they both nodded. Quickly, Rachel climbed off her bike.

"We'll fly up there and try to grab the petal," Pippa whispered with a wave of her wand.

Rachel and Kirsty felt a rush of excitement as a cloud of crimson sparkles transformed them into fairies. Silently fluttering their wings, the three friends flew up into the branches of the tree.

"There!" Pippa said softly, pointing
with her wand.

The goblins were sitting in a long line
on a sturdy branch. Their legs dangled
down. The biggest goblin was at the end,
holding the magic petal.

Rachel, who was closest, immediately
flew down and made a grab for it. But at
the last moment, the goblin saw her
coming and swatted her away.

"It's those pesky girls again!" he cried
furiously. "Do something!"

"I'll cast a really powerful spell," yelled
the goblin with the wand. "Uh, um . . ."

"Hurry up!" shouted the biggest goblin
as the three fairies flitted around him,
trying to grab the petal.

"OK, I've got it," replied the goblin
with the wand. "To escape these girls

would be quite nice —" he began,
shaking the wand.

"Nice!" shouted the biggest goblin
angrily. "It would be amazing! Not
just nice!"

"I don't know any words that rhyme
with 'amazing!'" the goblin with the
wand said miserably. Pippa and the girls
laughed.

"To escape these girls would be quite nice," the goblin said again, pointing the wand at the ground. "I demand an icy slide. I mean — I demand a slide of ice!" he finished.

Immediately, a huge chute of ice appeared, running from the branches of the tree to the grass below. One by one, the goblins jumped onto it with gleeful shrieks and slid to the ground. The biggest goblin took one last swipe at

Pippa and the girls before he followed his friends down the slide.

"They're escaping with the magic petal!" Kirsty cried as the goblins dashed away.

Petal Perfection

Pippa and the girls flew down from the tree as the goblins raced up a nearby hill. With an easy flick of her wand, Pippa made Rachel and Kirsty human-sized again. Then the girls jumped on their bikes.

"After them!" Rachel cried.

The girls zoomed off behind the

goblins, with Pippa riding in the basket
on the front of Rachel's bike. They
reached the foot of the hill really quickly,
but then they began to struggle.

"It's hard to pedal uphill!" Kirsty
panted, straining to go faster.

Pippa leaned out of the basket
and waved her wand. Dazzling
poppy-red sparkles swirled down onto
both bikes' wheels.

"Oh," Rachel yelled happily, "I'm going much faster now!"

"Me, too," Kirsty agreed. "Thanks, Pippa!"

With the help of fairy magic, the girls started gaining on the goblins.

"We're going to overtake the goblins soon," called Rachel.

"Let's try to grab the petal as we pass them," Kirsty suggested.

"Look, the goblin with the petal is a little behind the others," Pippa pointed out.

"Kirsty, I'll ride past on his right side, and you ride past on his left," Rachel said. "Then he can't escape."

"Good plan," Kirsty said, nodding.

As the two girls came up behind the goblin, Rachel went right and Kirsty went left. The goblin was clutching the petal in his right hand, and Rachel reached out for it as she rode up behind him.

But at the last moment, the goblin spotted her. "Trying to trick me?" he jeered. "You'll have to try harder than that!" And, laughing gleefully, he switched the petal from his right hand to his left.

Just then, Kirsty sailed past on the other side of the goblin. She reached out and grabbed the petal from his hand while the goblin was still laughing at Rachel.

"Hooray!" Pippa cried, as they raced past the other goblins.

"Hey!" shouted the big goblin angrily. "Give that magic petal back!"

The other goblins had now realized what had happened, but they were too late.

Rachel and Kirsty were speeding away on their bikes. Behind them, they could hear the goblins shouting and arguing with each other because they'd lost the magic petal.

"Girls, I can never thank you enough," Pippa announced as they finally came full circle and arrived back at the park gates. "Now all my poppies and lovely red flowers will bloom beautifully again," she went on. "I must take my petal back to Fairyland where it belongs."

She waved her wand over the petal, and it immediately shrank back to its Fairyland size. Pippa took the petal from Kirsty's hand and smiled. "Good-bye, girls," she cried, "and good luck finding the other petals."

Rachel and Kirsty waved as Pippa disappeared in a burst of poppy-red sparkles.

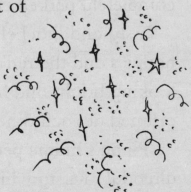

"Another magic petal found," Kirsty said happily. "Now we'd better get back to Blossom Hall!"

"Ooh, let's pick out our flowers from the shop first!" Rachel reminded her.

The girls rode back to Petal Perfection.

Kate was looking much happier when they walked in. "Hello again," she called cheerfully. "Look at my flowers. Some of them have completely perked up since you left."

Kirsty and Rachel could see that all the poppies and the red flowers were now looking bright and healthy. The girls grinned at each other.

"Pippa's magic petal is working again already!" Kirsty whispered.

"Tell me which flowers you'd like," said Kate. "You have more to choose from now."

The girls chose red and orange poppies, and Kate made them up into two pretty bouquets. Then Rachel and Kirsty said good-bye and biked back to Blossom Hall.

"Look, Rachel," said Kirsty, "all the poppies in the field are blooming again!"

"Don't they look beautiful?" Rachel said happily, looking at the silky crimson clusters nodding in the warm breeze. "I'm so glad we helped another Petal Fairy today."

"Now we can look forward to tomorrow!" Kirsty said with a smile.

RAINBOW
magic™

THE PETAL FAIRIES

Now Pippa the Poppy Fairy has her
magic petal back. Next, Rachel
and Kirsty must help

Louise

the Lily Fairy!

Take a look at their next adventure
in this special sneak peek!

Woodland Walk

"Blossom Lake, this way!" Rachel
Walker called out, seeing the wooden
sign ahead. Buttons, her dog, trotted by
her side. He paused to sniff at the trees
and bushes along the way.

Kirsty Tate smiled at her best friend,
Rachel. The girls were taking a nature
walk with their parents. Buttons started

to speed up as they turned onto the trail, heading deep into the woods.

"I can't wait to see the lake," Kirsty said, as she, Rachel and Buttons led the way down a sloping path through the trees. "There was a picture in Mom's guidebook, and it looked really pretty."

Rachel grinned at Kirsty. "I wonder what else we'll see today," she said quietly.

Kirsty knew exactly what her friend meant. "Oh, I really hope we meet another Petal Fairy," she whispered. "But remember what the fairy queen always says — we have to wait for the magic to come to us!"

There's magic in every book!

The Rainbow Fairies
Books #1-7

The Weather Fairies
Books #1-7

The Jewel Fairies
Books #1-7

The Pet Fairies
Books #1-7

The Fun Day Fairies
Books #1-7

SCHOLASTIC

www.scholastic.com
www.rainbowmagiconline.com

FAIRY3